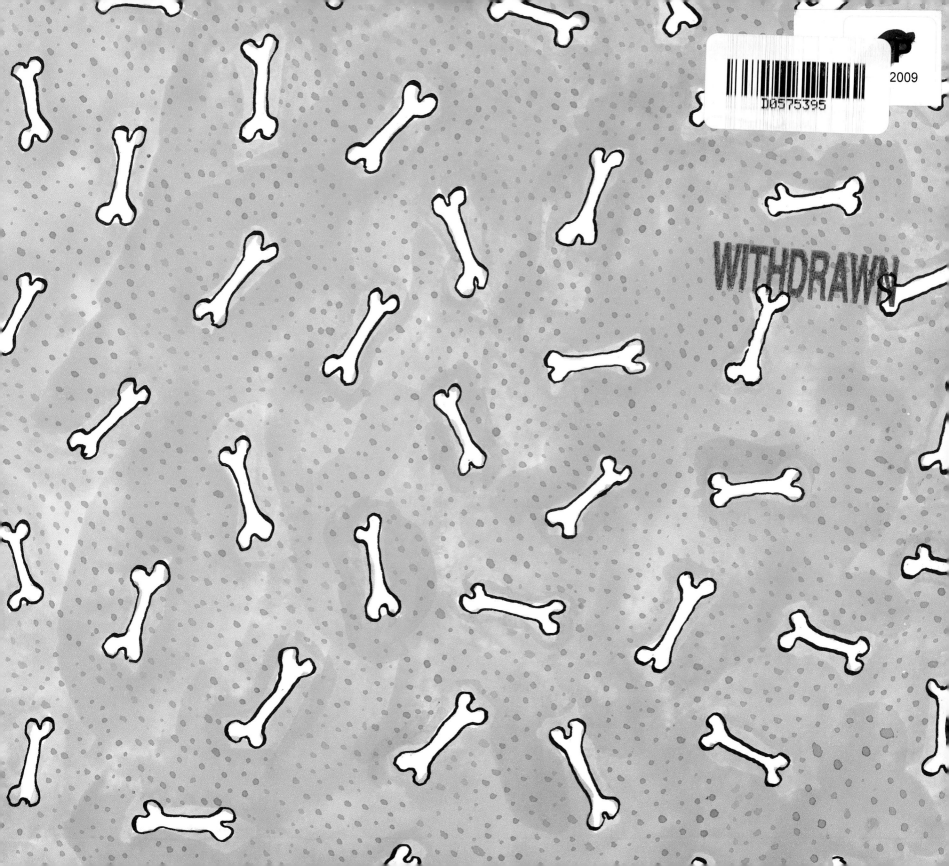

# Benny

First American Edition 2003
by Kane/Miller Book Publishers
La Jolla, California

Originally published by Lemniscaat b.v. Rotterdam

Kane/Miller Book Publishers
P.O. Box 8515
La Jolla, CA 92038
www.kanemiller.com

Library of Congress Control Number: 2002112324

Printed and bound in Singapore by Tien Wah Press, Pte. Ltd.

1 2 3 4 5 6 7 8 9 10
ISBN 1-929132-43-3

# Benny

By Sieb Posthuma

**Kane/Miller**
BOOK PUBLISHERS

Benny can't find his bone. He's sniffed everywhere.

He can't understand it.
Where could it be?

No matter where he
looks, no matter
how deep he digs,
it's nowhere to be
found.

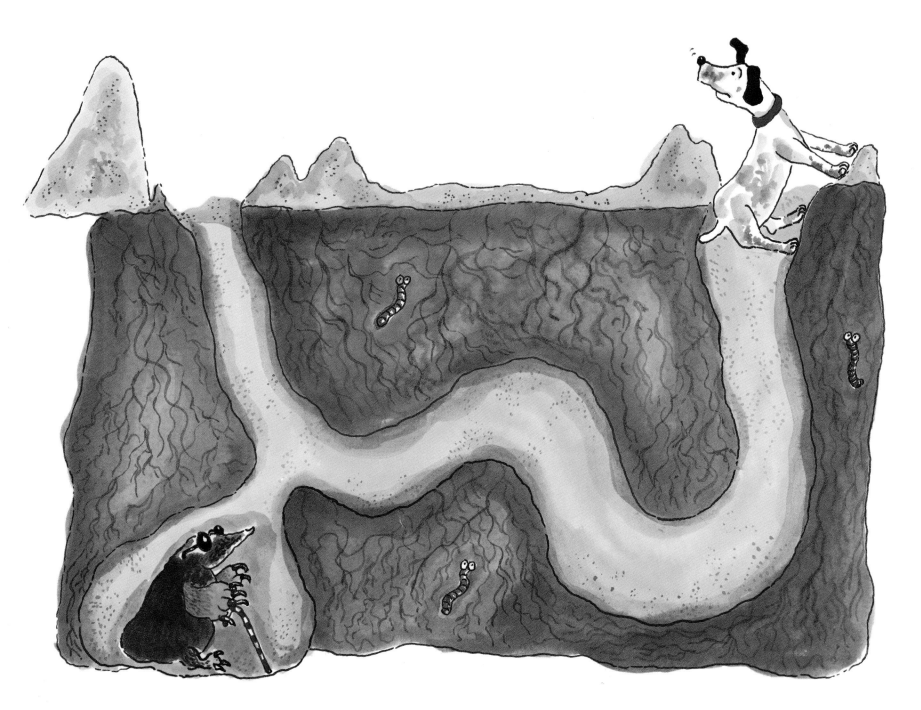

"I've really sniffed everywhere," he thinks.

The bone is Benny's favorite. He's never lost it before.
Without the bone, life is no fun.

Slowly, Benny heads for home.

"Don't you think my flowers smell lovely?" asks Mrs. Dash.

"They look lovely," Benny says, "but I don't smell a thing."

"Benny!  No treat today?" asks Spot.

Benny sniffs.  How strange.  That delicious bakery smell is gone.

At home, it's no better.
He sniffs frantically.

He can't smell the leathery old boots,

the musty box,

the soap bubbles,

the stale air,

the wonderful, filthy dog poop,

or the fresh, tart apples.

All the smells are gone.

Benny can't even smell his mother's special pie.

He can't smell anything.

"If you don't want any pie," Benny's mom says, "something must be wrong."

"Let's go see the doctor."

"What seems to be the trouble?" Dr. Duncan asks.

"I can't smell any smells," answers Benny.

"Say ahhhhhh." Dr. Duncan looks at Benny's throat.
"Hmm," he says.

"I think we'd better try the Sniff Machine."

"It's nothing serious," the doctor says. "He has a little cold. Keep him warm.

Steam will help, too. And rest, of course. Plenty of rest. He'll be better in no time."

Benny's mom tucks him into bed with a nice hot water bottle.

Benny stays in bed for two days and two nights...

Then something wonderful gets him up. Benny runs into the kitchen. "Mmm, bacon!"

His mom laughs. "You sound like your old self again."

He smells the flowers,

the apples,

the delicious bakery smell, and...

...Exactly where he buried his bone.
At last!

He rushes home to tell his mom the good news.

He snuggles on her lap.

She smells better than anything else in the whole world.

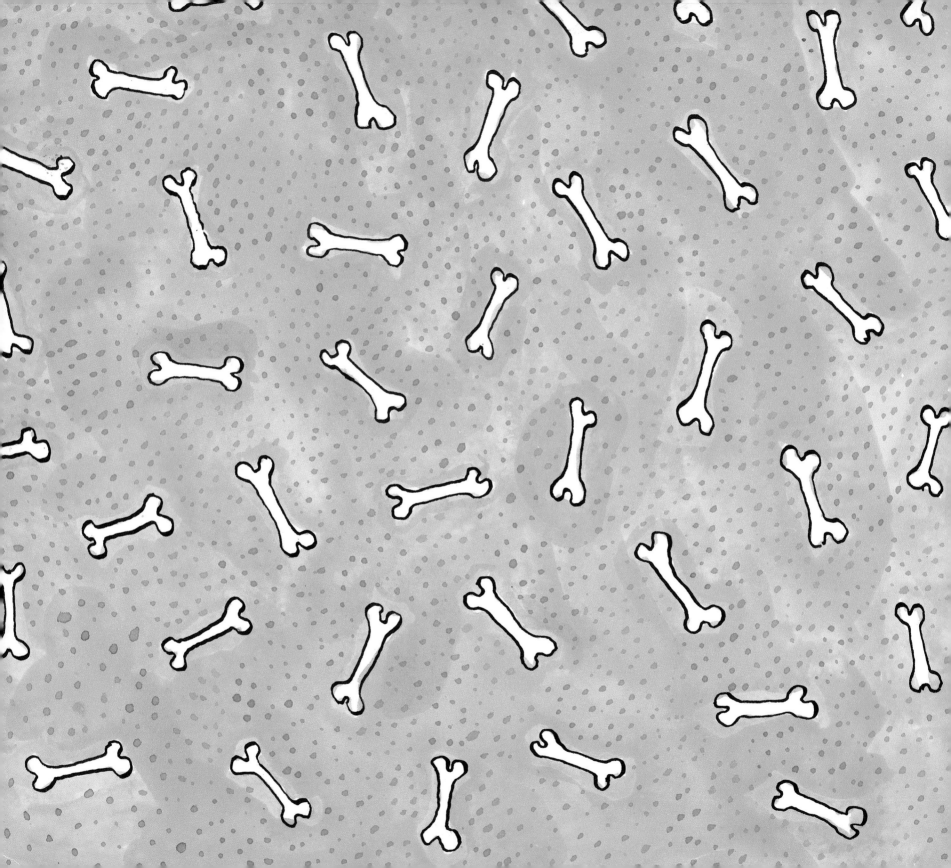